PUFFIN BOOKS

Frank Rodgers has written and illustrated a
wide range of books for children – picture
books, story books, non-fiction and novels.
His children's stories have been broadcast
on radio and TV and he has created a
sitcom series for CBBC based on his book
The Intergalactic Kitchen. His recent work
for Puffin includes the *Eyetooth* books and
the bestselling *Witch's Dog* and *Robodog*
titles. He was an art teacher before
becoming an author and
illustrator and lives in
Glasgow with his wife.
He has two grown-up
children.

Frank Rodgers

The
Bunk-Bed
Bus

PUFFIN

PUFFIN BOOKS

Published by the Penguin Group
Penguin Books Ltd, 80 Strand, London WC2R 0RL, England
Penguin Group (USA), Inc., 375 Hudson Street, New York, New York 10014, USA
Penguin Books Australia Ltd, 250 Camberwell Road, Camberwell, Victoria 3124, Australia
Penguin Books Canada Ltd, 10 Alcorn Avenue, Toronto, Ontario, Canada M4V 3B2
Penguin Books India (P) Ltd, 11 Community Centre, Panchsheel Park, New Delhi – 110 017, India
Penguin Group (NZ), cnr Airborne and Rosedale Roads, Albany, Auckland 1310, New Zealand
Penguin Books (South Africa) (Pty) Ltd, 24 Sturdee Avenue, Rosebank 2196, South Africa

Penguin Books Ltd, Registered Offices: 80 Strand, London WC2R 0RL, England

www.penguin.com

First published in Viking Kestrel 1989
Published in Picture Puffin 1991
Published in this edition 2004
3 5 7 9 10 8 6 4 2

Copyright © Frank Rodgers, 2004
All rights reserved

Set in 15/22pt Times New Roman Schoolbook

The moral right of the author/illustrator has been asserted

Printed in China by Midas Printing Ltd

British Library Cataloguing in Publication Data
A CIP catalogue record for this book is available from the British Library

ISBN-13: 978-0-141-31561-4

ISBN-10: 0-141-31561-X

J anet's and Sam's granny was full of energy.

Every morning she put on the tracksuit that she had knitted for herself and went jogging. Janet and Sam could hardly keep up with her!

Granny liked to say, "You're only as old as you feel . . . and I feel great!"

Another of Granny's favourite sayings was, "You're never too old to learn."

So she learned to work with wood and made shelves for Mum's collection of old plates.

She learned how to weld metal and
fixed Dad's car when it had almost
fallen apart.

Mrs Grimbly-Whyte, the snooty
next-door neighbour, didn't think much
of Granny's efforts. "Working with one's
hands is so unladylike!" she sniffed.

But Granny didn't mind what Mrs Grimbly-Whyte said.

When Janet's and Sam's old beds fell apart (after they had been using them as trampolines), Granny told them that she'd make new ones.

And she did!
She made brand new bunk beds.
Janet and Sam were delighted.

"The bunk beds will be terrific for
playing on," said Sam.

"As long as you don't play
trampolines," said Granny with
a grin.

So Janet and Sam pretended that
the bunk bed was a bus.

Janet drew a large sign that said . . .

The
Bunk - Bed
- BUS -
Trips to the
seaside.
ALL ABOARD!

"Coming, Granny?" asked Janet, holding out a ticket.

Granny laughed and said, "I'll come for a trip on your bus later, but just now I've got some work to do in the yard." And off she bustled.

Out in the yard, Granny put
Janet's and Sam's old iron bedsteads
beside all the other odds and ends
she had collected.

There were bits of old cars, rusty railings, an old washing machine, a staircase, tyres, wheels, railway signals and lots of wood.

She put on her welding goggles and started to mend Sam's old bike.

Just then Mrs Grimbly-Whyte
looked into the yard.

"My! What a lot of old junk you
have lying around, Mrs Jones," she
cooed. "Why don't you give it all to
the scrap man?"

"It might come in useful one day," said Granny. "You never know."

"That old rubbish? I doubt it!" sniffed Mrs Grimbly-Whyte.

"I spend my time doing much more ladylike things."

"This is my painting of my husband, Albert. I'm taking it to the Grand Art Exhibition at the Town Hall."

"Pity you're not artistic like me, Mrs Jones," sneered Mrs Grimbly-Whyte.

"But, of course, you never will be because you're too old now." And with that, she gave a nasty little laugh and flounced off.

Granny was furious! "Too old?"
she said. "Too old! What a cheek!"

Just then, Janet and Sam came into
the yard.

"Hello, Gran," said Janet.
"Can you come for a
trip on our bunk-bed
bus now?"

Granny's eyes lit up.

"Bunk-bed bus!"
she exclaimed.
"That's it! I'll
show her!"

And to Sam's and Janet's surprise,
she rushed off into the garage.

All day long, Granny worked in the garage, hammering and sawing and welding. The next day was the same.

Then, at about two o'clock, the noise suddenly stopped.

Out came Granny.

"It's finished!" she said, and flung
open the garage doors.

Inside was an amazing object.

"I made it out of your old bedsteads and other useful bits and pieces I had lying around," said Granny.

"It's a bus!" exclaimed Sam.

"A REAL bunk-bed bus!" Janet laughed.

"Gran, you are clever!"

21

Granny smiled proudly. "It's my sculpture for the Grand Art Exhibition," she said. "It starts at half past two, so there's no time to lose.

Come on, give me a hand!"

The family pushed Granny's
bunk-bed bus out of the yard . . .

and down the High Street.

It soon became a procession as all
the children from round about came
running to see Granny's wonderful
metal sculpture.

But when they got to the Town
Hall there was a disappointment in
store. The bunk-bed bus was too big
to go inside.

"Sorry, madam," said the doorman, "but you'll have to leave it in the courtyard."

"Oh, no," said Granny. "Now I won't be able to take part in the art exhibition."

She sat down on
the steps, looking
miserable.

Janet and Sam
looked at each
other.

"We must
do something,"
whispered Janet.

"Let's go inside," said Sam.

So when no one was looking, they
slipped through the doors.

In the main gallery the judges were
examining the exhibits – paintings
and sculptures of all shapes and sizes.

Mr and Mrs Grimbly-Whyte
stood smirking on either side of
Mrs Grimbly-Whyte's portrait of
her husband.

They obviously thought it was the
best thing in the whole exhibition.

They were convinced it was going
to win first prize!

Then one of the judges stepped up to the microphone and cleared his throat. He was going to name the winners!

Janet could bear it no longer. She
ran into the hall.

"Wait!" she shouted.

Everyone turned to see who had
disturbed the proceedings.

Mrs Grimbly-Whyte didn't want
anything to spoil her winning
moment, so she shouted, "No children
allowed. Throw
them out!"

But Janet and Sam ran up on to
the stage and whispered in the judge's
ear. The judge smiled . . .

then he turned and spoke into the
microphone.

"Ladies and gentlemen," he said.
"It seems that an exhibit has been
overlooked. Please come with me."

Followed by Janet and Sam and
the curious audience, he led the way
outside.

In the courtyard stood Granny's
bunk-bed bus, covered with children.

They were having a wonderful time.

The judges quickly put their heads
together . . .

and agreed that this was the best
piece of work in the whole exhibition!

They gave Granny first prize. She was delighted!

"How long have you been an artist, Mrs Jones?" asked the main judge.

"Since yesterday," said Granny.
"I always feel you're never too old
to learn."

"How true," said the judge, "how
true."

Mrs Grimbly-Whyte was green!
Her oil painting of her husband,
Albert, hadn't even been mentioned.

She was even greener when the
Town Council bought Granny's
bunk-bed bus and installed it in the
play park.

Granny was very proud, and with the money she bought something for everyone in the family.

A new hat for Mum, a new jumper for Dad . . .

new bikes for Janet and Sam . . .

. . . and a new tracksuit and welding mask for herself.

"Perhaps next time I'll build a ship," said Granny.

The family didn't laugh because they knew that with Granny . . .

. . . nothing was impossible.